W9-BLJ-736

This book is
your passport
into time.

Can you survive
in the Age
of Dinosaurs?
Turn the page
to find out.

TIME MACHINE 22

The Last of the Dinosaurs

by Peter Lerangis
illustrated by
Doug Henderson

A Byron Preiss Book

BANTAM BOOKS
TORONTO · NEW YORK · LONDON · SYDNEY · AUCKLAND

To Peter G. Hayes,
for his friendship, interest, and help

Time Machine readers:
Where would you like to go in the Time Machine?
You can write us at:
Byron Preiss Visual Publications, Inc.
24 West 25th St., 12th floor
New York, N.Y. 10010

RL 4, IL age 10 and up

LAST OF THE DINOSAURS
A Bantam Book/February 1988

*Special thanks to Judy Gitenstein, Carrie Sorokoff,
Jim Walsh, Bruce Stevenson, and Robin Stevenson.*

*Book design by Alex Jay
Cover painting by Mark Hallett
Cover design by Alex Jay
Mechanicals by Mary LeCleir
Typesetting by David E. Seham Associates, Inc.*

Editor: Ruth Ashby

*"Time Machine" is a trademark of
Byron Preiss Visual Publications, Inc.*

Registered in U.S. Patent and Trademark Office.

ISBN 0-553-27007-9

Published simultaneously in the United States and Canada

PRINTED IN THE UNITED STATES OF AMERICA

0 9 8 7 6 5 4 3 2

ATTENTION
TIME TRAVELER!

This book is your time machine. Do not read it through from beginning to end. In a moment you will receive a mission, a special task that will take you to another time period. As you face the dangers of history, the Time Machine will often give you options of where to go or what to do.

This book also contains a Data Bank to tell you about the age you are going to visit. You can use this Data Bank to help you make your choices. Or you can take your chances without reading it. It is up to you to decide.

In the back of this book is a Data File. It contains hints to help you if you are not sure what choice to make. The following symbol appears next to any choices for which there is a hint in the Data File.

To complete your mission as quickly as possible, you may wish to use the Data Bank and the Data File together.

There is one correct end to this Time Machine mission. You must reach it or risk being stranded in time!

THE FOUR RULES OF TIME TRAVEL

As you begin your mission, you must observe the following rules. Time Travelers who do not follow these rules risk being stranded in time.

1.
You must not kill any person or animal.

2.
You must not try to change history. Do not leave anything from the future in the past.

3.
You must not take anybody when you jump in time. Avoid disappearing in a way that scares people or makes them suspicious.

4.
You must follow instructions given to you by the Time Machine. You must choose from the options given to you by the Time Machine.

YOUR MISSION

Your mission is to travel to the end of the dinosaur era and find the last living dinosaurs.

For 180 million years, the dinosaurs ruled the land. Then, about 65 million years ago, they seemed to vanish all at once—leaving no survivors! To this day, no one knows why. Many scientists believe they disappeared gradually, from disease or weather changes. Others have evidence that it happened suddenly, after a huge asteroid or comet smashed into the Earth.

If you can locate the Earth's last living dinosaurs, you may help solve an age-old puzzle—the mass extinction of the greatest animals that ever roamed the Earth. To prove that you've found the last of these creatures, you must bring back a dinosaur tooth!

 To activate the Time Machine, turn the page.

TIME TRAVEL ACTIVATED.
Stand by for Equipment.

EQUIPMENT

On your mission to prehistoric times, you will need very rugged clothing. You will need to take your strongest, most waterproof boots and a compass—but travel light! Much of the Earth is covered by water in the Mesozoic era, and you don't want to be bogged down if you need to swim.

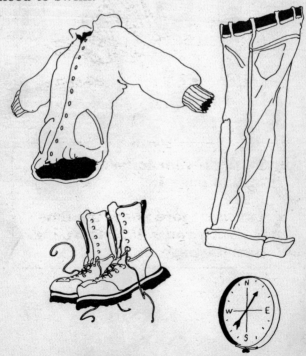

There won't be anything you can eat in pre-historic times, so you will need to bring quick-energy food that will last a long time in your pocket—such as granola bars, beef jerky, and candy.

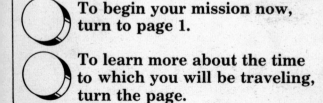

To begin your mission now, turn to page 1.

To learn more about the time to which you will be traveling, turn the page.

DATA BANK

1. The dinosaurs were very successful. *Before* they existed, the mammal-like reptiles who were our ancestors grew and thrived on the Earth. But after the dinosaurs took over, those early mammals were only able to evolve into small, primitive creatures! And the dinosaurs actually survived two early extinctions—at the end of the Triassic and the Jurassic.

2. Dinosaurs varied in size and speed. Some could look over a two-story house, yet others were as small as a turkey. And although some plodded along slowly, many could run at forty miles an hour!

3. Dinosaurs shed their teeth regularly, and new ones grew in to replace them.

The timeline and pictures on the next ten pages will give you an idea of life before the dinosaur age, when fish and mammal-like creatures shared the Earth with amphibians who could live in water and on land, and of life during the dinosaur age.

TIMELINE

million years B.C.

4600	Origin of Earth
3500-590	Early life forms
590-408	First fish
408-360	First land plants; first animals
360-286	**COAL AGE** —first amphibians
286-248	**PERMIAN AGE** *Early*—first reptiles *Mid-to-Late*—first mammal-like creatures
	(Extinction)

MESOZOIC AGE: AGE OF THE DINOSAURS	248-213	**TRIASSIC PERIOD** *Early*—first dinosaurs (but mammals dominate) *Mid-to-Late*—dinosaurs dominate for first time
		(Extinction)
	213-144	**JURASSIC PERIOD**
		(Extinction)
	144-65	**CRETACEOUS PERIOD**

	(Extinction)
65-2	**TERTIARY PERIOD** —hoofed mammals and apes
2-present	**QUATERNARY PERIOD** —human beings

Remember: for prehistoric times, the higher the number, the farther back in time! For example, 200 million B.C. is longer ago than 65 million B.C.

ichthyostega

COAL AGE
(360-286 million years B.C.)
The *ichthyostega* was one of the first amphibians. It was so primitive it hadn't even developed ears!

dimetrodon

eryops

diplocaulus

PERMIAN AGE
(286-248 million years B.C.)

This is the last age before the dinosaurs—*none* of the creatures on this page is a dinosaur.

Early—Fin-backed reptiles and other amphibians ruled the earth.

PERMIAN AGE
(286-248 million years B.C.)

Late—Fin-backs became extinct and mammal-like reptiles, such as the head-butting *tapinocephalus*, took over. These reptiles probably developed into the mammals we know today.

erythrosuchus

cynognathus

TRIASSIC PERIOD
(248-213 million years B.C.)

The *cynognathus* is thought to be the ancestor of all mammals, including humans. Throughout the first half of this period, mammals and dinosaurs were fighting for dominance. Most dinosaurs were meat-eaters.

Until the mid-Triassic, all creatures had legs that pointed outward from the hip, as do the legs of lizards and crocodiles, today.

labels within image: pterosaurs, brontosaurus, megalosaurus

JURASSIC PERIOD
(213-144 million years B.C.)
By this period, the dinosaurs were the major plant- and meat-eaters on Earth.

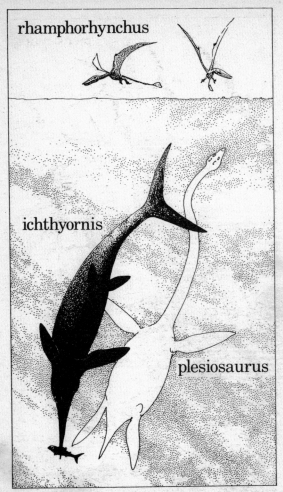

rhamphorhynchus

ichthyornis

plesiosaurus

All dinosaurs from this point on had legs that went straight down from the hips and pointed forward.

styracosaurus

hypsilophodon

albertosaurus

dienonychus

pteranodon

CRETACEOUS PERIOD
(144-65 million years B.C.)
This was the last and greatest dinosaur era,
with duck-billed dinosaurs, horned and armored dinosaurs, and fearsome tyrannosaurs.

THE EARTH IN THE CRETACEOUS PERIOD

To understand the end of the dinosaurs, it will be helpful to know how the world was changing during the Cretaceous period.

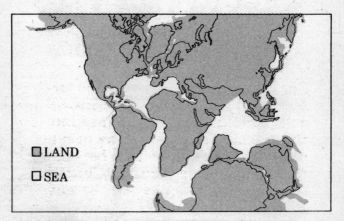

LAND

SEA

THE WORLD IN THE MIDDLE OF THE CRETACEOUS

The continents are moving away from each other. The Rocky Mountains have formed, and a shallow, warm sea has covered the middle of North America since the Jurassic period. In fact, the whole planet is warm, even the areas near the North and South poles.

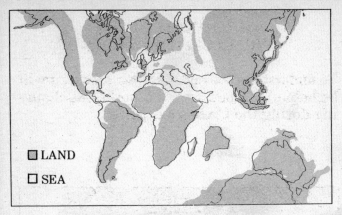

THE WORLD AT THE END OF THE CRETACEOUS

The continents have moved even farther apart. The Rockies have eroded, and the inland sea has drained into the ocean. This makes the ocean colder and deeper; the land becomes colder, too. A strip of land has formed to connect what's now Alaska and Russia.

DATA BANK COMPLETED. TURN THE PAGE TO BEGIN YOUR MISSION.

 Don't forget, when you see this symbol, you can check the Data File in the back of the book for a hint.

ot bad. You've found a great spot—right in the middle of a bed of pine needles. It's as soft as a mattress, but the needles are huge, the size of fingers. You're in prehistoric times, but you're not exactly sure where or when.

Crash! Without warning, a pine tree falls to the ground and just misses your head. You roll away quickly and spring to your feet. Looking around, you see you're in a pine forest, but most of the trees seem to be dying.

Suddenly you feel the ground shake. Spinning around, you see a huge pile of fallen logs and branches. Beyond it you hear crashing noises. Hoping to see whatever is making the noise, you climb up on top of the pile.

Your eyes widen as you catch a glimpse of your first dinosaur—from your Data Bank, you recognize it as a flesh-eating *megalosaurus!* It's staggering from side to side and bumping against trees. The poor thing is so weak it can hardly walk.

But that "poor thing" is thirty feet long, with gleaming, jagged teeth and sharp claws on its toes and fingers. And it just caught a whiff of fresh meat—you!

You turn to run, but your foot gets caught. All at once, the entire pile of logs rolls out from under you and sends you tumbling downward. As you hit the ground, a furry animal the size of a wolf scurries out from beneath the pile and into the woods.

Brushing yourself off, you look back and see that the pile of logs was actually covering something up—an enormous gray mass with wrinkled skin. You realize you were standing on top of a dead *brontosaurus*.

Its teeth flashing, the megalosaurus now pokes its head over the dead dinosaur, and you turn to run. But the megalosaurus stops at the body of the brontosaurus and starts to eat.

You turn away from the disgusting sight. As you survey the desolate area around you, something occurs to you. Weak and dying dinosaurs, falling trees—it looks as if you've traveled to the end of the last dinosaur period, the Cretaceous. You may have already completed your mission! Maybe that megalosaurus is the last living dinosaur.

You snoop around on the ground to see if you can find a tooth that has broken loose. There are no teeth, but there *is* a claw. You stoop to pick it up—and you notice two beady eyes staring at you. It's the mammal that ran out from under the log pile. It seems to realize the competition is too stiff for the brontosaurus meat, and it's sizing you up instead! You freeze in terror as it charges toward you with its long canine teeth gleaming. The only way for you to escape is to quickly jump in time!

 Escape 10 million years into the future. Turn to page 10.

ou run to the cave and hide inside. The duck-billed dinosaur is still there, pacing back and forth near her nest. Her eyes are focused toward the mouth of the cave, as if she's afraid that the albertosaurus might enter.

You stay by the mouth of the cave and peer outside. The albertosaurus slowly approaches the styracosaurus, then lunges at it with its snapping jaws. The low-lying enemy dodges away.

For a few minutes, the two beasts just circle around each other. Standing erect on powerful legs, the albertosaurus has a definite advantage in size. But the four-legged dinosaur is a good match—it lowers its head and rams one of its spikes into the bullying beast. The albertosaurus roars in agony and lifts its clawed foot to push the other dinosaur away.

Suddenly an ear-splitting trumpet noise fills the cave. You cover your ears and turn around to see the duck-billed dinosaur in a frenzy. Small, ratlike mammals with sharp teeth are attacking the unhatched eggs and devouring the unborn dinosaurs inside.

The duck-bill swats at the little animals with her forelegs. Some of them run away, and some of them run in between your legs and sniff your shoes. Outside, the albertosaurus and its foe are rolling toward the cave. The ground below you is rumbling.

More than anything else, you want to jump out of here and travel to a safer period of time!

 Head 140 million years ahead to the twentieth century. Turn to page 19.

You find yourself next to a large striped tent. It's nighttime and you're freezing.

Maybe you can sneak inside the tent to warm up. It's lit on the inside, and people are walking in through the front. You notice that someone is checking invitations at the entrance.

A horse and carriage pulls up beside you, and a man jumps out. In his rush, he drops his invitation. You pick it up. It's shaped like the wing of a *pterodactyl,* and engraved on it are the words: YOUR PRESENCE IS REQUESTED AT A CELEBRATION FOR THE NEW YEAR 1854.

You give it to the man, who is searching his pockets in vain. Then you tiptoe around to the back of the tent. You see that waiters and busboys are rushing from inside the tent to a supply carriage; they're going through an open tent flap. You grab a plate of food and sneak through.

You can't believe what you see. About twenty grown men with serious faces and long coats are sitting down to a formal dinner—inside a huge, bizarre-looking statue of a four-legged monster with its back removed! You can't figure out what it's supposed to be; it looks like a fat, giant iguana, but it has a horn on its nose.

"Don't just stand there!" the head waiter says to you. "Serve Professor Owen!" He points to a distinguished-looking gray-haired man. You pick up a steaming plate of roast beef. In order to put it in front of Owen, you have to walk around the creature and reach inside.

Just as you do so, a man stands up and bangs his fork on a glass to quiet everyone down. "Gentlemen," he says, "I would like to introduce the world's greatest dinosaur expert, Professor Richard Owen."

To a round of applause, Owen rises up. He's at the head of the table—which is inside the head of the monster.

"Take his food back," the head waiter whispers to you. "We'll keep it warm while he speaks."

But you're too interested in hearing Owen speak to pay attention to the food.

"Thank you," Owen says, "but truly we are here to toast two other men. First, to the memory of Dr. Gideon Mantell, who discovered the teeth and bones of the great iguanodon . . ."

You smile as the men all cheer. So Mantell really *did* find a dinosaur tooth, after all!

". . . and second, to the brilliant work of Mr. Benjamin Waterhouse Hawkins, who has been building this wonderfully accurate model of the iguanodon, in which we are now sitting!"

There's more applause as Hawkins takes a bow. You have a feeling that this "wonderfully accurate" statue is all wrong—it doesn't look a thing like any of the dinosaurs you know about, especially with that little horn on its nose. The paleontologists have a long way to go in their research, but they'll realize that in a few years.

All of a sudden you're grabbed by the shoulder. The headwaiter yanks you around and puts his face right up against yours. "I asked you to return the roast beef!" he hisses. When he gets a close look at your face, he seems shocked. "Say, I never hired you! What are you doing here, disrupting my staff?" He looks around and shouts, "Police!"

By now, people at the table are staring at you. You slip out the open tent flap and into the night.

This would be a good time to find out what a *real* iguanodon looks like.

 Hop back 140 million years to the Early Cretaceous. Turn to page 25.

It's much quieter here, but it's also much darker. A few feet away from you, there's a cracking sound. Your eyes slowly adjust, and you realize you're in a cave.

You look toward the cracking sound and see a flat, circular mound of dirt. Inside it are eggs the size of a chicken's, and one of them is hatching. You go over to look; it'll be interesting to see what kind of creatures existed 10 million years after the dinosaurs died out.

Heonnnk! A deafening sound, like the loudest car horn you've ever heard, blasts through the cave. You spin around to face a large green dinosaur with a mouth that looks like a duck bill—it's a *parasaurolophus*. It's snorting at you through a long, stiff tube on its head. And it looks angry.

What's a *dinosaur* doing here? you wonder. According to your calculations, all of them are supposed to be dead.

You run to a corner of the cave, where the duck-billed dinosaur can't reach you. Can it be that this huge creature is the mother of

those little eggs? You watch as the hatching egg finally cracks open. Sure enough, a tiny dinosaur struggles to its feet. It's a pigeon-sized replica of the mother.

You wonder how this dinosaur and her children survived the extinction. Maybe they're the only ones that did. This could be a great discovery.

While the mother is busy with her newly hatched offspring, you are able to move slowly and quietly along the wall of the cave. As soon as you are past the dinosaur, you dash toward the opening.

Outside, you see a field of grasses surrounded by a forest of small ferns. Among the grasses are bizarre, colorful flowers with large petals. You've never seen or smelled anything like them. Their scent is so strong that they make you sneeze. The noise startles a pack of small animals who race away from a small brown lump in the grass and into a hole.

You notice the animals look a lot like mammals. In fact, they remind you of the animal you saw 10 million years earlier—except these are smaller. That's strange; you'd expect mammals to evolve into *larger* animals after the dinosaurs were out of the way. After all, this *is* the Age of Mammals—isn't it?

You go into the forest to see if you can find any other mammals. You just hope the little creatures don't bite.

In an instant, you realize it doesn't matter,

because lumbering toward you through the trees is a towering *albertosaurus* with a mouthful of sharp teeth! This is one dinosaur you definitely want to avoid!

Quickly you run the other way, but now you're in the path of another dinosaur! This one is on all fours and has thick, sharp horns sticking out of a crest around its neck. You recognize it as a *styracosaurus*.

With a sinking feeling, you realize that you're not in the Age of Mammals at all. The destruction you saw 10 million years ago must have been the extinction in one of the *earlier* dinosaur periods, the Jurassic. You're in the Cretaceous, now—and you're in big trouble.

You could slip back into the cave with the parasaurolophus. You could escape to a time you *know* is safe—the twentieth century.

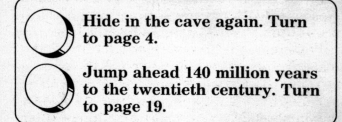

Hide in the cave again. Turn to page 4.

Jump ahead 140 million years to the twentieth century. Turn to page 19.

ou are in a long, musty room that has eleven dark wooden desks. From where you're standing, you can see that each one has a complete supply of quill pens, paper, and rulers. On the desk closest to you is a French newspaper dated May 19, 1824.

You look around the room. Hanging from the walls are detailed drawings of creatures that resemble dinosaurs. But when you get closer to them, you see that the drawings are all wrong. The "dinosaurs" all look like giant horned lizards, with legs that go out to their sides from each hip, and bellies that slink near the ground—they're nothing like the creatures you've seen.

Crrrreeeeaak! A tall, carved-wood door swings open into the room. A fat older man in expensive-looking clothes enters. Behind him is an energetic man who looks young enough to be his son.

"Baron Cuvier!" the young man says loudly. "I believe there's a burglar here!"

You've been caught. Thinking fast, you grab a rag that's on the floor and start dusting off one of the desks.

"Morning, sirs!" you say merrily. "Quite a bit of dust today. I'll be taking my lunch break soon."

Cuvier nods and looks back to the younger man. "You were saying, Sir Charles?"

"With all due respect, Baron Cuvier," says Sir Charles, looking embarrassed, "I think you may be taking the easy way out by saying that the ancient living things died off because of a sudden catastrophe!"

" 'Due respect' is something you should have been showing me all along!" Baron Cuvier answers. "I can't *tell* you how many times people have come up to me and said, 'Sir Charles Lyell thinks you are being ridiculous. He says the ancient creatures died off gradually.' " He sneers at the younger man. "A man of my scientific reputation does not appreciate gossip."

Cuvier and Lyell continue quarreling. You notice that neither of them has actually said *dinosaur*—the word probably hasn't been invented yet. But even so, their argument does sound a lot like the one the scientists were having over 160 years later. The balding scientist at the conference was right!

A knock on the door interrupts the two men. In walks a dark, quiet man holding an object that looks like a giant tooth.

"Ah, Dr. Mantell," Cuvier says, looking annoyed. "Do come in."

"Excuse me for interrupting, Baron," Mantell says. He seems impressed by the room.

"You certainly have quite a few assistants," he says, looking at all the desks.

Cuvier raises an eyebrow as if insulted. "All the desks belong to me—one for each of my interests. Now how may I help you, Doctor?"

Mantell holds out the tooth. "This is the specimen I was telling you about. My wife found it. I'm sure it belongs to one of the giant creatures you've spoken about."

Baron Cuvier pulls a magnifying glass from his pocket, grabs the tooth, and examines it quickly. "I thank you for your keen interest in fossils, Mr. Mantell," he says. "But this is clearly a rhinoceros tooth."

With that, Cuvier turns to continue his discussion with Lyell. Mantell starts to protest, but instead he sulks away. By the look on his face, you can tell he knows he's right.

You think so too.

"Don't ignore him!" you blurt out to Cuvier and Lyell. "He knows what he's talking about!"

Oops. You shouldn't have opened your mouth.

"I beg your pardon!" Cuvier says, staring at you in anger. "I believe you were hired to *clean!* Perhaps you would like to leave right now—and never come back!"

He grabs you by the scruff of your neck and pushes you into the hallway, then slams the door behind you.

At the end of the hall, Mantell is starting

to walk down a flight of stairs. He smiles at you and winks. He must have heard you.

As he descends out of sight, you wonder how you can find out if he was right. Maybe people in the next generation know. Or maybe you'd better go to the twentieth century to pick up information—by *then* it should be easy to find out.

 Travel thirty years into the future. Turn to page 7.

 Travel ahead to the twentieth century. Turn to page 32.

You're tumbling down a long, dark chute. Your flailing arms and legs clank against metal walls. With a *thud*, you hit bottom.

A narrow tunnel stretches out in front of you. In the distance is a small square of light. Icy cold air whooshes around you and makes you shiver as you crawl toward the light. You see the square is a metal grating. Soon you hear voices.

You pull yourself up to the grating and look out into a hallway. You realize you must be in an air-conditioning duct.

On the wall is a sign that says NATIONAL CONVENTION OF PALEONTOLOGISTS, with an arrow pointing right. Those voices must all belong to dinosaur experts!

There's no one in the hallway. Quietly, you give the grating a push—and it pops right out of the wall! You grab it before it falls.

You lower yourself into the hallway and head toward the voices, which are coming from a room behind a set of huge wooden doors.

"The evidence is all there!" you hear a loud voice say. "It was a comet that hit the earth at the end of the dinosaur era—"

This conference is right up your alley. You brush yourself off and walk in.

The door creaks as you open it, but nobody notices. Of the twenty-five people seated around an oval table, it seems half are trying to speak, and the other half are furiously taking notes.

The voice you heard belongs to a fiery, dark-haired man. On the wall behind him is a chart of the solar system. He continues, "I believe that the sun has a companion star, which we call Nemesis. Every twenty-six million years, Nemesis comes close to the sun—"

He turns to the chart and points to a strange band of white beyond Pluto. "This is called the Oort cloud," he says, "and it's full of comets. When Nemesis passed by at the end of the Cretaceous era, its gravity must have pulled a comet into a collision course with Earth!"

You run the three dinosaur eras through your mind, to refresh your memory: Triassic was the earliest, Jurassic was the middle, and Cretaceous was the last.

"And the comet crash would have sent up a cloud of dust that circled the world and kept it in darkness, right?" a woman asks.

"Exactly," the man says excitedly. "Then all

the plants died out from lack of sunlight, so the plant-eating dinosaurs starved—"

"And when *they* died, the meat-eaters would have had nothing to eat . . ." a gray-haired man in a tweed jacket says, nodding thoughtfully. "I don't know, it sounds too far-fetched. . . ."

You're intrigued by the dark-haired scientist. "What's your proof of the Nemesis theory?" you ask him.

"We have soil samples from the Cretaceous era that show a huge amount of *iridium* in the soil, from the exact time the dinosaurs died off—and iridium is a substance found in meteors and comets!"

You scratch your chin. Something doesn't sound right. "But if the Earth was hit by a comet," you say, "then why didn't the mammals die too?"

"Good question!" a bearded man says, standing up. "I think the answer has to do with the Great Plains of America. They were covered by warm seas during the Jurassic period, but we know the seas drained into the ocean during the Cretaceous. Clearly, temperatures got colder, causing the dinosaurs to die off gradually . . ."

"Pardon me," a red-haired woman interrupts, "but they died off because temperatures got *hotter!*"

"Not exactly," another woman says. "The draining seas caused a land bridge to form between what's now Alaska and Russia. Then dinosaurs could travel from one continent to the next—spreading new diseases. *That's* how they died!"

Your comment has touched off a debate. Every scientist in the room seems convinced that he or she has the best theory to explain the Great Extinction. They're talking so fast you only pick up snatches:

". . . yes, dust and soot did block the sun, but *volcanoes* caused it, not a comet! The continents were moving away from each other during the Cretaceous period, and as the land shifted, volcanoes opened up . . ."

". . . they were killed by poisonous flowers that evolved in the Cretaceous . . ."

". . . magnetic reversal! The South and North poles switched, and that took away the atmosphere's protection from the sun's harmful rays. The dinosaurs were sunburned to death!"

". . . rats ate their eggs . . ."

You realize that the scientists don't really know what happened. There seem to be two main groups—one that thinks the dinosaurs died off suddenly, and the other that thinks it happened slowly, over many years.

You keep asking questions, trying to figure

out whose theory makes the most sense. But none of the arguments seems foolproof. You'll just have to travel through time to find the real reason yourself.

At one point, a small, balding man turns to you with a smirk and says, "You know, we really don't know any more about the Great Extinction than we did a hundred and sixty years ago, when the dinosaurs were first discovered."

You wonder if he's right. Suddenly you feel a hand on your shoulder. You spin around to see a burly man in a security-guard uniform. He motions you to follow him to the doorway.

"You're awfully young to be a paleontologist, aren't you?" he says. You smile innocently and nod.

"May I see your I.D.?" he continues.

"Uh . . ." You fumble through your pockets. "I must have left it—"

"In the air-conditioning duct?" he says, his voice dripping with sarcasm. He pulls the broken grating out from behind the door and holds it in front of your face.

You gulp deeply and feel cold sweat forming around your collar.

"Clever little vandal, aren't you?" the guard says. He looks at the dinosaur claw that you still have in your hand. "Have you stolen something from the museum?"

You start to back away toward the exit. "Museum? N-no! I . . . er . . . just lost my way looking for—" At that moment, you break away from him and run down the hallway. The last thing you want to do is explain yourself.

You've got to escape into time, but you're torn. Should you search elsewhere in the twentieth century for someone who really knows the answer to the Great Extinction?

Or was the balding scientist telling the truth?

Jump back one week to look for someone who knows the answer to the extinction. Turn to page 32.

Jump back 160 years to see if the balding scientist was right. Turn to page 14.

The first thing you notice is a sweet scent floating through the air. You're surrounded by tall evergreens, and between the trees are strange, colorful flowers with thick petals and sturdy stems. You take a deep breath. The flowers are like nothing you've ever seen or smelled before. Dragonflies the size of bats are hovering around them.

To your right, the trees end near a body of water that looks like a large lake or a sea. You walk over to the shore and see the water lapping over the skeleton of a long-necked dinosaur half-covered with sand. The world seems very quiet. Maybe, by accident, you've arrived after the Great Extinction.

No such luck. Through the forest comes the sound of thundering footsteps. You swing around to see a giant, scaly hand wrap itself around a tree trunk. But the hand isn't like any hand you've seen before. In place of a thumb, there's a spike—a spike that looks strangely familiar to you. In a flash you realize why: it's exactly like the horn that was on the *head* of the iguanodon model at the 1854 New Year's party!

But you don't feel much joy at discovering Benjamin Waterhouse Hawkins's mistake. You've met a real iguanodon, all right—but it's about to attack you, and that spike looks sharp!

The moment you turn to run, you're jerked upward, as if you were on an elevator. You look down and see that you're standing on a curved platform of metal plates. Long, sharp spikes stick out of the platform's sides.

Raaahhhhhggggghhh! The platform roars. Your face goes pale as you realize you're standing on the back of an armor-plated *ankylosaurus!*

You hang on for dear life as the four-legged ankylosaurus charges toward the iguanodon. This fight ought to be pretty spectacular—but you'd rather not be a participant!

You'd better get out of here fast. But you want to get on with your mission and figure out exactly when the Great Extinction occurred. A trip to the twentieth century might give you some clues.

Travel 120 million years ahead into the twentieth century.
Turn to page 32.

Your feet splash through the ravine as you run away at top speed. You hear the crashing of bushes and small trees behind you as the boulder rolls right over them. In seconds you'll be completely—

Oof! Before you know what's happened, you're underwater. You've fallen into a deep, narrow hole in the ravine, and the boulder rolls harmlessly over you.

You hold your breath as you hear the rumbling recede into the distance. Carefully, you pop your head above the surface. Ten feet away, you see a shallow, rocky stream that winds up and out of the ravine. You slowly make your way up the stream against the current.

Before long, you're out of the ravine and ascending a hill. When you get to the top, you gaze out over the ravaged surroundings. Maybe from here you can see what caused this destruction.

It's hard to miss it. Smoke is billowing out of a hole that looks a mile wide.

Is this the crater left by the collision of a comet or asteroid with Earth? If it is, you've solved one of the greatest mysteries of natural history!

Wait a minute. A crater this big is likely to remain through the ages. But you've never heard of anything like it in modern times. Where could this possibly be?

If you travel ahead to the twentieth century and stay in this same location, you'll find out.

Go 65 million years ahead.
Turn to page 53.

hhhooooosshhh! You duck away as a fireball zooms by your head. It lands at the bottom of a tree, which immediately goes up in flames. In seconds, the dry grass around it catches fire—and it starts to spread right toward you!

You turn and run like crazy. But you'll have to compete with about twenty duck-billed dinosaurs. They're running toward you away from the tree and blowing their horns frantically.

If the dinosaurs don't get you, the fire will. Your lungs feel as if they want to burst as you race to your right toward a steep, soot-covered hill. You fling yourself into a deep ravine at the base.

The duck-bills stampede by, and you sit tight—the ground around you is too wet to be affected by the fire. Feeling a little safer, you look around at the landscape. You've never seen so much destruction. Under a blackened sky, the ground is littered with the bodies of dead tyrannosaurs, triceratopses, and duck-bills. Deafening explosions fill the air.

You must be near the Great Extinction! These types of dinosaurs all lived during the Late Cretaceous, and this is definitely a major catastrophe. Now all you need to do is find a tooth and scram.

You put one hand to your mouth and wave the smoke away as you search the ground. You know from the Data Bank that dinosaurs shed their teeth regularly, because they always have replacements growing underneath. Surely you can find one or two here.

But it may not be so easy. Barreling down the hill and about to turn you into a prehistoric pancake is a tremendous boulder!

You look up and see flames dancing at the top of the ravine. You'll just have to outrun the boulder.

If you can escape, you'll be able to learn more about the Great Extinction. But if you jump into the future, you at least know you'll be alive!

You must decide what to do. Time is running out.

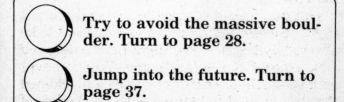

Try to avoid the massive boulder. Turn to page 28.

Jump into the future. Turn to page 37.

You can't see a thing. There's a muffled din of voices around you, and the air is stuffy. You grope around in the dark.

Thud. The ground is so soft and springy that you lose your footing. You tumble downward and fall against a door, which flies open. You land in a huge, brightly lit room.

"Are you all right?" a voice asks. "What were you doing in a closet full of wrestling mats?"

You look up to see a dark-haired girl staring at you with an amused smile. Behind her, dozens of people are milling among exhibits set up on tables. Strung between two basketball hoops above you is a banner that says: SIXTH GRADE SCIENCE FAIR.

"This is a gymnasium," you say under your breath.

"Brilliant deduction, Watson!" the girl says. "Do you have an exhibit?"

"An exhibit . . . ? Er . . . no," you answer, picking yourself off the floor.

"Well, then pull yourself together and look at mine!" She points to a table covered with

models of dinosaurs. "I call it Deena's Dinosaurs!" She grins and shows you her nametag, which says, "HI! I'M DEENA KRILLBORN!"

You pick up a strange-looking model of a pink reptile with wings. *"Pink?"* you say.

"Some scientists think so," Deena says. "Pink flamingos get their color from the red algae they eat from the sea, which is exactly what these pterosaurs ate!"

You wonder if you can pick up some information about the Great Extinction. Before you can ask, Deena starts talking:

"My exhibit begins with the discovery of an iguanodon claw by Gideon Mantell, which at that time was believed to be a tooth. I then examine the evolution of dinosaurs—right on through the Great Extinction—"

"Uh, excuse, me," you say, "I have some questions about the extinction—"

"Excellent!" she says, practically jumping with excitement. "My research shows that evolution may have a lot to do with that." She points to a picture of a creature with a large, corrugated fin on its back. The fin looks like a sail.

"This is a *dimetrodon,*" she says. "It's *not* a dinosaur. You know how you can tell the difference?"

Before you can answer, Deena continues. "First of all, it's an amphibian, which means it could live both in water and on land. Second, it was slow-moving and cold-blooded—many scientists think dinosaurs were warm-blooded. But the most obvious thing is its legs. Its thighs go out to the side from the hip, as with lizards or crocodiles. Dinosaurs evolved into upright walkers, with legs pointed straight ahead!"

"Yes, but the Great Extinc—"

"I'm getting to that!" Deena says with an edge of impatience. You'd better let her talk. "The giant amphibians became extinct when a tougher, speedier breed took over—*our* ancestors, the mammal-like reptiles!" She smiles with pride. You humor her by smiling back—and hope she gets to the point.

"Then suddenly the dinosaurs appeared," she says. "Over the next one hundred and eighty million years, they evolved into hundreds of species, large and small. All our mammal ancestors must have been killed off— but for some reason, the smallest ones survived."

"So if some small mammals lived through the whole dinosaur age, then how did they survive the Great Extinction?"

"Well, it must have something to do with evolution! Maybe the mammals were just smarter. Maybe they ate the dinosaurs' eggs. . . ."

"So the answer is to learn more about evolution," you say, half to yourself.

Deena's face turns red. You can see she took your comment as an insult. "I suppose you could do better!" she retorts, putting her hands on her hips. "I spent three months on this exhibit! Look at the quality of my models!"

As she walks over to one of her dinosaur statues, you back toward the exit. You really didn't want to get into an argument.

"Thanks, Deena! Gotta go!" you say. You're intrigued by what she said about evolution, but you'd rather try to find the Great Extinction right away.

Try 65 million years into the past. Turn to page 30.

A fiery object hurtles out of the black sky toward you. You hit the ground. The object hits you squarely in the face—but not before it turns into a huge cake of soot.

Coughing, you brush away the soot from your face. You look around—it doesn't seem as if you went anywhere! The sky is just as dark, and the same explosions are resounding. Could this be the end of the Great Extinction? You look around for dinosaurs, but you see none.

Through the haze you catch the outline of moving figures. But they're not dinosaurs— they're *people!* Most of them are dark-skinned, thinly clad, and panicked. They're running right toward you, and it doesn't look as if they intend to stop.

One of them spots you and cries, "Krakatoa! Krakatoa!" He gestures into the distance behind him and pulls you along.

You look over your shoulder and stop in your tracks. A deep rumble shakes the ground, and through the thick atmosphere you can make out a monstrous, glowing cone—the Krakatoa volcano!

This looks similar to what you just saw; maybe the Great Extinction was caused by a volcano, not by a comet!

As red flames spit out of the top, a voice pierces the darkness:

"Come on, mate! Get into this boat or you won't live to see 1884!"

But you're frozen in shock. Racing right toward you at top speed is a steaming, bubbling lava flow.

Time to go—but to where? Maybe you'd better heed the advice you were given before— try to learn about the Great Extinction by observing evolution. At least it'll be safer.

Making sure that you can't be seen through the haze, you quickly jump to the Permian period to see the creatures that existed before the dinosaurs.

 Jump 265 million years into the past. Turn to page 43.

ock! . . . Bock!
Coming from beyond a distant ridge are noises that sound like batting practice for a baseball team, only the sounds are louder and deeper. You may be 30 million years in the future, but the swamp—and the smell of ammonia—have lingered the whole time.

You decide to see what's over the ridge. As you approach, the stench recedes into the distance. But the noise becomes louder.

You reach the top of the ridge and look over. Two huge, scaly-skinned animals are fighting to the death. You're glad you're safely above them.

But not for long. The ground gives way below you, and you slide down a muddy incline. When you land at the bottom, you're ten feet away from the sparring creatures.

Up close they're even more fearsome. They look something like buffalo, but their heads remind you of bowling balls—round and thick, covered with tight, shiny skin.

As the animals circle around each other, you can practically feel their hot breath. You consider trying to go around them. But if they notice you, you're in trouble. So you sit tight and watch.

You remember from your Data Bank that they are *tapinocephaluses,* reptiles who probably evolved into mammals. You brace yourself as they charge toward each other, heads lowered.

Thwock! The sound echoes against the ridge as the two heads make contact. One of the animals falls to the ground.

Suddenly you realize you're not alone. Lurking in the shadows is a low, sinister figure—slinky as a reptile but shaped like a wolf. As it comes into the sun, you see the glint of two enormous, sharp, tusklike teeth.

Without warning, the wolf-reptile attacks the victorious tapinocephalus. The larger creature roars threateningly, but the wolf-reptile knows that its adversary has been weakened in the fight. It digs its fangs into the tapinocephalus's leg. Instead of fighting back, the tapinocephalus just shakes itself loose and hobbles away.

Now the wolf-reptile starts over toward the *dead* tapinocephalus. You begin to tiptoe away.

Too late. The wolf-reptile sees you. With a sound that's between a shriek and a bark, it speeds your way.

You try to run but slip in the mud. The wolf-reptile stands over you and bares its fangs.

But all it does is nuzzle you with its snout. You squirm away, but the animal won't stop. It's tickling you!

Before long, you're rolling on the ground with laughter. You realize that the wolf-reptile is sniffing at your pocket. You reach inside and pull out a couple of strands of beef jerky.

Snap! Barely missing your fingers, the wolf-reptile devours the jerky and walks away.

You breathe a sigh of relief. But something puzzles you. Ferocious mammals are all around you; it looks as if they've inherited the Earth from the fin-backs. And yet the dinosaur age is about to come and wipe them away. What was it about the dinosaurs that made them able to take over the land from the mammals during the Mesozoic period?

By jumping ahead 20 million years, you may be able to see what became of the mammals at the beginning of the dinosaur age.

 Turn to page 50.

ccch! The smell of ammonia is overpowering. You put your hand to your nose and look around. You're surrounded by a prehistoric swamp. You try to walk over to the edge of it, but your legs are knee-deep in slime.

There's someone else in the swamp, and he doesn't seem to mind the smell. Lounging on top of a rock in the swamp is a familiar-looking animal. Along its spine is a huge curved fin that looks like a sail. You remember where you've seen it before—at Deena's science fair exhibit. It's a dimetrodon, a reptile that lived long before the dinosaurs.

Sure enough, just as Deena said, its legs go outward from the hip, not straight down, as with those of the dinosaurs you've seen.

You notice something else that makes it different from the other dinosaurs—this creature seems like a real slowpoke! It's just sitting there motionlessly, eyeing the water. Instead of hunting, it's waiting for its prey to come to it.

In the water, a few feet from the dimetrodon, a group of bizarre-looking amphibians can't seem to stop swimming into each other. Their

44

heads are shaped like boomerangs, and because their eyes are on top, they can't see where they're going!

You can't help but laugh at them. But your smile is instantly wiped away by the sight of a hideous, flat-headed amphibian walking toward the swamp. It's an *eryops,* and it's about as big as the dimetrodon.

You jump away, but it's not interested in you. It plops into the water and snags a fish.

The dimetrodon remains still. You begin to think it's in a coma.

But not for long. As soon as the eryops comes to the middle of the swamp, the dimetrodon pounces! Slashing viciously with its claws and digging its sharp teeth into the amphibian, the dimetrodon has itself a large, quick meal.

Then, just as before, the fin-back climbs onto its rock again and rests, absolutely still.

These creatures are much more primitive than dinosaurs, but just as scary. You're curious to see how the dinosaurs may have taken over from them—but you're not exactly sure how far ahead to go. You also want to get away from the stench.

**Jump ahead 30 million years.
Turn to page 40.**

**Jump ahead 50 million years.
Turn to page 50.**

t's too dark for you to see. You're leaning against a smooth, flat surface. You slowly move your hand along until your finger hits a switch. You flick it up and immediately you are blinded by light. Blinking, you step back and bump into someone behind you.

"Excuse me," you start to say as you turn around, "I didn't mean to—"

Suddenly you're speechless. You're eye-to-eye with a hideous humanoid that has bulging eyes, leathery skin, and fingers like claws! You try to escape through the door, but it's locked. You look back to see the creature standing stock-still and staring at you.

"Uh . . . I come in p-peace!" you stammer. But the humanoid says nothing. At that moment you hear voices beyond the wall of your small room.

"Welcome to the Canadian National Museum of Natural Sciences," you hear a man say.

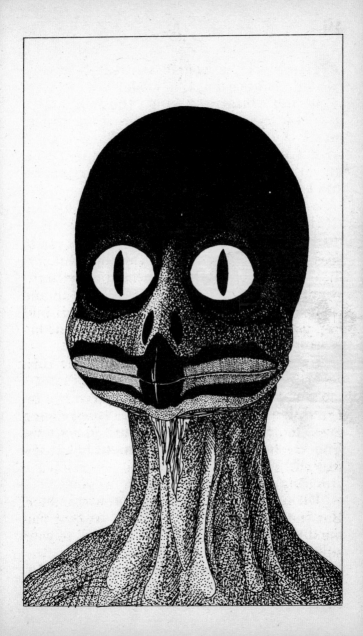

"Thank you," a woman answers. "I'm very excited about seeing this model."

"It's quite bizarre-looking," the man continues. "But you must remember, it was made mostly by educated guessing. The professor tried to imagine what a dinosaur might look like if it had survived the Great Extinction and evolved to the present day."

So *that's* what you're looking at—a model!

"Honestly, though," the woman says, "is it really possible that any of the dinosaurs would have been likely to develop intelligence?"

"Well, one of the last dinosaurs, the stenonychosaurus, had a brain area even larger than that of the mammals of the period. And its hands were thought to have thumbs for grasping!"

"Hmm. All the qualifications we see in the development of apes millions of years later," the woman says.

You look back at the statue. Its eyes are oval-shaped. Its nose and mouth jut out together like a beak, and each hand has three long, bony fingers.

A shudder goes through your body. You realize that if the Great Extinction hadn't happened, *these* creatures might be walking the Earth instead of humans!

The man and woman stop right outside the door, and you hear the fumbling of keys.

You must escape into time before anyone sees you. You have already observed evolution through the Permian and Triassic periods. You quickly decide that it's time to go to the next dinosaur period, the Jurassic.

Travel back 170 million years.
Turn to page 63.

You're in a thick, dark jungle. It's the Early Triassic period, millions of years after the dimetrodons became extinct. Maybe now that you've reached the dinosaur era you can see what it was about the first dinosaurs that made them able to start taking over the Earth.

You're about to get your answer. Crashing through the woods comes a furry animal that looks like an overgrown dog, only it has legs like a crocodile's and sharp fangs. It's a *cynognathus,* which some scientists think is an ancestor of all mammals, possibly even humans!

Chasing right behind it is one of the most fearsome creatures you've seen. It's about fifteen feet long, with a heavy, thick body. But the most frightening thing about it is its gigantic head, with a mouth so big it could fit you inside. This is an *erythrosuchus,* one of the very first dinosaurs.

Both creatures run close to the ground; their knees jut out to the side from their hips. You notice that neither of them has evolved the type of legs that the later dinosaurs had—legs that pointed forward instead of outward.

The erythrosuchus catches up to the smaller animal in a clearing not far away. The two creatures square off against each other. The cynognathus tries to bite its bigger and slower enemy.

At first you think the dinosaur seems too sluggish for the cynognathus. But as soon as it opens its mouth, you change your mind!

The cynognathus is no match for the snapping jaws of the dinosaur. With a couple of powerful lunges, the erythrosuchus rips into the helpless animal.

Now you can see why the early mammals lost out to the early dinosaurs. But you've heard that the cynognathus may be your ancestor—so what did it evolve into during the next 160 million years, while the dinosaurs took over? After all, it must be hard for a species to evolve when it's being dominated by bigger and stronger enemies!

You feel sorry for the cynognathus—but only until you turn to face another one staring at you. This one is alive—and drooling.

You yell in terror. The cynognathus stops and cocks its head.

"Don't come near me!" you scream, gesturing with your arms. The cynognathus backs off. You realize that the beast is afraid of you!

"Boooo-ah-ha-ha!" you shout—and the cynognathus scurries away, whimpering like a puppy.

You feel proud of yourself as you plot your

52

next move. You might pick up some clues about the Great Extinction if you follow the dinosaur's evolution into the next period, the Jurassic. But now you're curious about two other things: what was it about the dinosaurs that allowed the mammals to regain control after the Great Extinction? And what would have happened if the dinosaurs had survived to live in modern times? A twentieth-century scientist may be able to help you with that one.

 Jump ahead 50 million years to the Jurassic period. Turn to page 63.

 Jump ahead 160 million years to the end of the Mesozoic period. Turn to page 55.

 Jump ahead to the twentieth century. Turn to page 46.

This doesn't look at all like the place you left 65 million years ago! A plateau stretches out for miles around you.

Men in turbans and women wearing veils bustle back and forth. Several stores line the street. You go up to a shopkeeper who's standing outside a market. His face is deeply lined with age, but his alert eyes seem to size you right up.

"You're a tourist, no?" he says. "First time to India? How do you like the Deccan Plateau?"

This seems strange to you. There should be a crater here. Maybe the man can give you some sort of clue.

"Very well, thank you," you say. "I'm a student. Uh, maybe you could tell me a little about how the plateau was formed. . . . "

"Ah, a future geologist, I see!" the man says, nodding slowly. "Well, this area was actually once a field of lava. It was built up by millions of years of volcanic explosions."

Something starts to dawn on you. "When did the volcanoes start erupting?" you ask.

"Oh, about 65 million years ago, the experts tell me."

So it wasn't a crater that caused the damage that you saw. "Maybe a *volcano* caused the extinction!" you mutter to yourself.

The man overhears you. His face lights up. "Extinction?" he says. "So you're a student of prehistoric times, eh? I am, too. As a matter of fact, I've spoken to *all* of the dinosaur experts who've passed through here!"

"What have you learned about the Great Extinction?" you ask.

The man raises a gnarled finger to his mouth. "The land holds many secrets—secrets that must not be discussed." Then he looks you straight in the eye. "But I can tell you this: Always remember, one can only determine the end by examining the beginning. . . ." With that, he gives you a mysterious grin and shuffles inside his shop.

You scratch your head. What can he mean by this? Should you examine the time period *before* the dinosaur age to find a clue to your mission? Maybe he's saying what Deena said: the key is to learn more about evolution.

Travel back 280 million years to the Permian era, before the dinosaurs existed. Turn to page 43.

You're between two sand dunes. There's not that much around besides beach grass, but you hear the rushing sound of water nearby. You climb one of the dunes and look around. Not far away is a river.

As you walk toward the river, you notice strange little amphibians hopping and swimming. Most of them are unfamiliar, but some look like salamanders. Soon you catch a glimpse of a creature you've definitely seen before—a frog.

You wonder if you're quick enough to catch it. On tiptoe, you approach the frog. It stays perfectly still. You slowly lean over and reach down.

Your hand darts out quickly. But the frog is quicker. It slips away and disappears into the water, as you fall flat on your face.

You pick yourself up and laugh—until you hear a sinister hissing noise from behind a snaggly bush. A turkey-sized dinosaur with bulging eyes is giving you a look, as if scolding you for chasing away its meal. From your Data Bank, you recognize it as a *stenonychosaurus*,

one of the Late Cretaceous dinosaurs. It may
be small, but it looks pretty dangerous.

Something about it seems different from
other dinosaurs you've seen. Its head move-
ments are quicker, and its eyes seem to be sizing you up with more intelligence.

For a long time it just stands still, its big
eyes darting from side to side. Before long,
another frog hops near the water. The stenonychosaurus watches it but doesn't pounce.
Instead, it waits while a small animal appears
from behind a dune. The animal looks like a
dog, only it has huge, jutting canine teeth.

Which is going to be smarter, the mammal
or the dinosaur? you wonder.

The mammal slowly stalks the frog. But the
frog sees it and hops into the water. Quickly,
but a little too late, the mammal splashes into
the water after it.

The stenonychosaurus waits until the
mammal is in the river, and then it attacks.
The mammal is taken off guard, and it can't
run away too easily, because it's knee-deep in
water.

The little dinosaur and the mammal are a
pretty good match, but the stenonychosaurus's
strategy has given it an advantage. It's definitely a smarter hunter than other dinosaurs
you've seen. And its reward was a nice, juicy
mammal for dinner, instead of a little frog.

You're impressed at the stenonychosaurus's
craftiness. You wonder what would have hap-

pened if it had survived the Great Extinction. Would it have evolved higher intelligence, such as that of a human being? You're tempted to travel to the twentieth century to find out if any dinosaur expert knows. But you should also continue learning about evolution—since you *were* in the Triassic period, and your next stop should be the Jurassic.

Right now, though, the stenonychosaurus seems to be concentrating on food. It seems to want some dessert—and it's staring right at you!

Escape back 100 million years into the Jurassic period. Turn to page 63.

Escape to the twentieth century. Turn to page 46.

ou're prepared for a
swim this time. You hold your breath, close
your eyes, and start to wave your arms.

It's a good thing there are no humans
around, because if there were, they'd think
you looked ridiculous. Something seems to
have gone wrong. You're on solid ground—or
almost solid. It's the edge of a swamp.

You remember from your Data Bank that
the inland seas of America drained out to the
ocean in the Late Cretaceous. This swamp is
what's left of the huge body of water you almost drowned in during the Jurassic period.

You look down to see dozens of plesiosaurus
and sea lizard skeletons that have been picked
almost clean of flesh and muscle. This may be
a sign of the beginning of the Great Extinction! From one of the skeletons, a path of very
large footprints leads over a hill. There's still
a bit of meat on the bones, but a pack of little
animals is trying to finish it off. They're digging in with long, sharp teeth.

These ratlike creatures look familiar. They
remind you of the cynognathus you saw in the

Early Triassic period, but they're much smaller.

Suddenly you realize you've witnessed evolution at work. By now, the dinosaurs have been dominating for so many millions of years that they've forced the larger mammals into extinction. The only mammals that could survive and evolve were the smaller ones, who were able to run and hide. It reminds you of humans—we've been able to bring large animals, such as the buffalo, to the brink of extinction, but we have trouble getting rid of bugs and mice!

Your thoughts are interrupted by a flying reptile overhead. It's the strange-looking *pteranodon*. As it glides through the air you can tell it's much bigger than the pterosaurs you saw in the Jurassic period. In fact, it's the size of a small airplane! You can't imagine how it can possibly keep itself in the air. Not only are its wings enormous, but it has a head that extends straight back to a pointy tip. The head alone looks to be about eight feet long.

When the pteranodon swoops down toward you, you can see your whole life flash before your eyes.

You dive into some nearby bushes and cover your head. But the pteranodon isn't interested in you. It lands on the carcass and sends the furry animals running. Don't worry, you want to say to the mammals, your time will come.

Just then you're distracted by different

62

noises in the distance. Behind a grove of trees
you hear screeching. And over the hill, where
the large footprints lead, are loud, clanking
sounds. You're curious about the noises, but
exploring them may be dangerous. Which way
should you go?

 Go behind the trees. Turn to
page 68.

 Follow the footsteps over the
hill. Turn to page 78.

Maybe this wasn't such a great idea—you're in the middle of the sea! Salt water rushes into your mouth and nose as you struggle to keep yourself afloat.

As you gasp for air, you feel totally baffled. Even though you've just traveled in time, you expected to be in the same area you left—that is, on dry land!

All at once you realize what's going on. You remember that the middle of North America was completely covered by water in the Jurassic period.

You start doing a dog paddle and look around. A storm is brewing. The sky is turning shades of purple and gray, and whitecaps are whipping up around you. Thirty yards away, an enormous sea lizard jumps out of the water in a frenzy.

You know that sharks act that way when they sense food nearby, but what about sea lizards? You don't want to take any chances. Your arms plunge through the water as you swim toward the shore.

Suddenly you catch a glimpse of something hurtling through the sky above you. All you need now is for some prehistoric bird to pluck you up, you think, still paddling. You look up to see that it's not a bird at all. It's a terrible-looking reptile with wings—a *pterosaur!* Sharp buck teeth stick out of its mouth, and its long snout is pointed at the end. You watch the flying beast dive-bomb into the sea and spear a fish on its snout.

Things in this Jurassic sea don't look too promising. But the shore is only about fifty yards away now, so you keep swimming.

Just as you think you're going to make it, another bizarre creature pops its neck up out of the water . . . and up . . . and up. Its body is about ten feet long, but half of that length is its neck! You flounder around in the water and try to change your course. A *plesiosaurus* is not something you want to tangle with right now.

But the plesiosaurus doesn't seem interested in you, anyway. It moves slowly about, apparently looking for fish. You concentrate once again on the shore.

All of a sudden you hear wild thrashing in the water. It's the big sea lizard. It has clamped its jaw around the plesiosaurus's tail.

Your eyes widen as the sea lizard lifts the plesiosaurus clear out of the water. You see that the monster is at least twice as long as its prey—probably twenty-five feet! The size

of its jaws makes a shark seem as dangerous as a goldfish.

Faster than you thought possible, you swim to the sandy shoreline. You breathe a sigh of relief as you reach it, safe and sound, about ten feet away from a pink flamingo.

A pink flamingo? You rub your eyes and realize you're seeing a pterosaur exactly like the model Deena showed you. You're relieved to finally see a creature that seems pretty harmless.

You watch as it thrusts its long, narrow snout forward, like a sword, opening it to reveal a dense row of bristles instead of teeth. It dips its mouth into the water and uses the bristles to strain out its food—the microscopic red algae that give it that strange color!

You're amazed at how many different kinds of life there are in the Jurassic age. The creatures are much more advanced than they were in the Triassic period. And you know they'll just keep on evolving for millions of years.

Behind a boulder a few feet away you see a slight movement. It's a nasty-looking giant crocodile. You had better stop thinking about Jurassic life and think about your own. It's time to leave this era.

You realize you still haven't really picked up any clues about the Great Extinction. Maybe if you go on ahead to the Late Cretaceous, you'll figure out why you've been trying to observe evolution. But right now you could be in the Early *or* Late Jurassic period—so you're not exactly sure how far ahead to go!

If you're in the *Late* Jurassic, you'll need to travel 70 million years to hit the Late Cretaceous.

If you're in the *Early* Jurassic, you'll need to travel 150 million years to hit the Late Cretaceous.

Go ahead 150 million years.
Turn to page 74.

Go ahead 70 million years.
Turn to page 59.

You cover your ears as the loud screeching noises pierce the air. But the smell of the decaying body by the swamp is even more overpowering, so, moving quickly, you carefully follow the sounds behind the trees.

There you see a furious battle between two Late Cretaceous dinosaurs—a *deinonychus* and a *hypsilophodon*. The deinonychus is jumping into the air and tearing into its victim with huge, powerful claws on its hind feet. With each attack, it screams victoriously.

The hapless hypsilophodon can do little more than try to run away. Its claws aren't nearly as sharp, and when it opens its mouth you can see why it doesn't try to bite the deinonychus. There are no teeth at all in the front of its mouth, and only flat, plant-eating ones in back.

As the one-sided fight continues, you're struck by the deinonychus's appearance. It looks as if its body is covered with feathers, but you can't tell for sure, because it's moving too fast. And its claws and hopping movement

seem more like a bird's than a dinosaur's. You wonder if it's possible that some dinosaurs evolved into birds.

You're distracted by clanking noises that are coming from over the hill behind you. It sounds like a couple of dinosaurs working on a Late Cretaceous chain gang!

Investigate those sounds. Turn to page 78.

You're sliding down a sandy hill. You land in a heap at the bottom and feel the sun scorching against your cheeks. A breeze comes along, but it only seems to make you more uncomfortable.

Not far away, an abandoned pickup truck lies half-covered with sand—a sign of the twentieth century. There's not much you can learn about dinosaurs here, so you prepare to time-travel.

Just then, a gigantic shadow sweeps across the ground. Probably some eagle or hawk, you think.

Then you notice the shape of the shadow's head. It stretches back into a long, pointed tube. It *is* a dinosaur!

You rub your eyes as you look up to see a pteranodon. There's no mistaking it. It flaps its wings gracefully and moves its strange head from side to side. No one will ever believe this. You wish you had a camera.

Soon you notice that the pteranodon is losing steam. Its wings start to get caught in the wind, and it can't seem to hold itself up.

Your eyes widen as the enormous flying beast suddenly plunges downward. With a sickening crash, it hits the ground—and splits into pieces!

You hear voices from behind a small mesa. "It's down! It's down!"

Two men come running. They go over to the pteranodon and examine the wings. "It's going to be expensive," one of them says. "And we've already spent thousands of this model."

"Maybe it's impossible," the other man says with a sigh. "Maybe pteranodons never flew."

You know he's wrong, but you can't talk to him now about his model. You have to complete your mission. The only question is exactly how far back to go; each time before, you've always just missed the Great Extinction.

The two men are about to turn your way. Quickly, hop into time before they see you.

 Jump 65 and a half million years into the past. Turn to page 81.

 Jump 64 and a half million years into the past. Turn to page 107.

You're in a lush, wooded area. There's no water around, so you're safe from crocodiles and sea lizards. Wildflowers are all over the place; that means you must be in at least the Cretaceous period. Maybe you're near the time of the Great Extinction.

A rustling noise tips you off that something's nearby—probably something you'd rather not face. You look for a tree to climb.

Suddenly a six-foot-long reptile crashes through the undergrowth after you. By now you're an expert at escaping dinosaurs, and you scurry up a knotty tree.

The reptile waddles after you and stops at the bottom of the tree. Looking up at you, it flashes its teeth.

There's something about it that's not right. Its legs go out sideways from the hip, just like those of the very early dinosaurs in the Triassic period. But they're all extinct by the Cretaceous period! Maybe the scientists have been wrong all along, or maybe you've discovered some kind of Rip van Winkle dinosaur that's been asleep for millions of years.

Some other strange things catch your attention. You hear a sound a lot like the neighing of a horse. And not long after that, voices—*human* voices! How could there be humans in the Cretaceous period, you wonder, feeling confused. Could you have jumped too far in time?

"So tell me," a very polite voice says. "Is there much wildlife on Komodo Island?"

You spot a light-skinned man with a camera. Beside him is a dark man, who appears to be guiding the tourist through the jungle. The dark man stops in his tracks when he sees the reptile. *"Ora!"* he cries.

His companion is turned the other way and doesn't see anything dangerous. "Ora?" he says. He pulls a small book out of his pocket and flips the pages while muttering "Ora . . . ora . . . ah, here it is! *Ora* is another word for the fearsome Komodo Dragon—"

The tourist looks up and sees the Komodo Dragon. His face goes white with shock. The guide is already running back the way they came, and the tourist quickly follows.

But the reptile seems exhausted from its attack on you. It reminds you of the dimetrodon, who would lie still between attacks to gather strength. Dinosaurs never did that. You know now that you have traveled beyond the Cretaceous period and that this Komodo Dragon isn't a dinosaur. It must be some kind of giant reptile that somehow managed to survive the ages on this island. Maybe there aren't any other larger meat-eaters on the island to compete with it.

You look down to see it sleeping right at the base of your tree. Even though it seems harmless now, you don't feel that climbing down would be a smart idea.

You should probably get back to the Mesozoic period. You've just come from the Jurassic sea. If you go back to the same spot during the Cretaceous, you'll be able to see how the dinosaurs *and* the land evolved. Maybe that'll give you some clues to the Great Extinction.

Next stop is 120 million years into the past. Turn to page 59.

You sneak to the top of the hill and look over.

Your breath is taken away by the sight of the most vicious dinosaur of all—the Tyrannosaurus rex. It bellows in anger and lunges at a four-legged, spiked beast you recognize as a *nodosaur.*

Ca-chunk! The tyrannosaur's huge jaws have clamped down on its enemy. But the nodosaur's skin is as hard as a metal shell, and three gigantic, sharp tyrannosaur teeth break off and fly toward you.

One of them lands on the ground at the base of the hill. Your eyes light up. It may not really be the time of the Great Extinction now, but perhaps you can bring this tooth home to complete part of your mission.

Slowly you work your way down the hill. The battling dinosaurs are too busy to notice you . . . you hope.

The tooth is in the tyrannosaur's line of sight. You wait until it turns away, then you quickly tiptoe over to the tooth.

Your sudden movement causes the tyrannosaur to turn around. You feel yourself

starting to go numb as it bares its bloody teeth and runs toward you.

The next thing you know, you've scampered up a tall pine tree. You're well above the tyrannosaur now, but it's looking up at you hungrily.

You're surprised at how scrawny its arms are—they're far too small to shake you out of the tree.

"Pick on someone your own size, Rexy!" you shout down. You feel pretty safe and confident—until the nodosaur charges.

Hearing the footsteps, the tyrannosaur turns around and dodges out of the way. The nodosaur rams its spikes into your tree.

You scream as you're knocked off your branch and into the air. But there *is* something below you to break you fall—the tyrannosaur's back!

You cling onto it for dear life—from just below the tyrannosaur's neck. Its skin is green and leathery. From this close up, you can see that its jaws are as big as you are. And they're opening again, to prepare for another nodosaur attack.

This is a perfect time to resume your search for the Great Extinction—before *you* become extinct!

**Travel ahead 50 million years.
Turn to page 102.**

You're being swept along in the current of a deep river. Ahead of you is a deafening roar—you're approaching a waterfall! Quickly you swim crosscurrent toward a large green boulder on the riverbank. If you miss it, you're a goner.

With each stroke, you're headed farther downriver. It's going to be a matter of inches. . . .

You stretch your arm and, hurling your body toward the bank, you get a hold of the boulder. Breathing heavily, you pull yourself onto dry land.

You plop down on the rock to rest. Then you feel something peculiar. Either you're hallucinating from the tension of your adventures, or the rock moved! You turn around to examine the boulder—and a long head pops out to examine you! The "boulder" that saved your life is actually a prehistoric tortoise!

You're grateful, but you hop off and back away. The tortoise is as big as many of the dinosaurs you've seen, and the sharp ridge along its jaw looks dangerous.

You notice that you're still breathing heavily. By now you should be recovered. Your body starts to break out in a sweat, and you feel dizzy. Is it really that hot out? You look up. The sun *is* bright, but it's never made you feel like this before.

Suddenly you're whacked across the back. You lurch up into the air and crash to the ground. Behind you is a crested, duck-billed dinosaur, wobbling along on its hind legs as if it were drunk. It's having as bad a day as you are.

The only way to explain the weather is to assume that you must have landed near the equator. But you don't want to stick around. Maybe the weather would be more pleasant farther north.

Before you look at your compass, you scan the area. The sky is hazy but free of soot. A couple of other duck-bills wander around in a funk, and a triceratops is having a hard time standing up. But they're all still alive. This must be before the Great Extinction.

Judging from these dinosaurs, though, it may not be a long way off.

The best thing to do, you think, is to time-travel just a few years ahead. You look at your compass to make sure you're headed north.

Something's wrong. The needle is going wild. This must be the time of "magnetic reversal" that you heard about at the paleontologists' convention. For some reason, the

South Pole and the North Pole are switching magnetic charges. And while it happens, the Earth isn't protected from the sun's harmful ultraviolet rays!

If you don't get out now, you'll be fried to death. Already you feel as if you're about to keel over. Without stopping to think, you jump into time.

Go into the future. Turn to page 91.

Go into the past. Turn to page 88.

You run after the ichthyornis as it flies over the ridge. But you can't go very fast, because you have to step around all the dinosaur bodies in the way. Finally you reach the top. It's a steep ledge that looks over a long canyon. The canyon winds into the distance, which makes you suspect that this was once a deep, mighty river. The air is a little clearer at the bottom, and you see more dinosaur corpses strewn all around.

But at least some of them are alive down there. You lower yourself into the canyon to see if you can find the ichthyornis.

This isn't going to be easy. The wall of the ridge drops straight down to the bottom. The only way you'll be able to make it is by grabbing onto the roots that are sticking out of the soil.

Slowly you climb down. There are lots of holes in the dirt, and you dig your boots into each one. Both of your hands clutch onto the strong roots.

Reeeeeaaaak! You're halfway to the bottom when you hear a loud squeal. You look down.

A mammal the size of a large rat has popped out of a hole and has sunk its teeth into your boot. You shout in horror and try to shake it off.

Suddenly your grip loosens, and your hands slip off the root. You tumble down the rest of the way and land on the bottom.

You feel bruised and sore, and there are two big holes in your shoes. But at least you've gotten rid of the little creature. It seems strange that even though the dinosaurs are dying, this small mammal had energy to spare. Maybe the mammals survived this disaster by hiding in holes. The dinosaurs may have dominated the Earth for 160 million years or so, but it's the little mammals who are going to evolve into the next era.

You realize that learning about evolution *has* helped you understand the Great Extinction.

As you glance around, you can see hundreds of furry animals gnawing on dead dinosaur bodies. It's a regular smorgasbord—triceratops for lunch, tyrannosaur for dinner. . . .

In the midst of it all is a live triceratops, sitting over a nest of eggs. Most of them have hatched, but the baby dinosaurs have died instantly. Still, some of the eggs are whole—and the ichthyornis is lurking nearby, eyeing them hungrily. Obviously the candy bar wasn't enough.

The triceratops mother can barely stand,

but she defiantly faces the feathered attacker. The ichthyornis flaps its wings and lunges for the nest, but all the triceratops has to do is lower her head, and the ichthyornis backs away from the sharp horn above her nose.

You feel pity for the triceratops and the other dinosaurs. You wonder how all this destruction was caused. It's awfully cool—that's probably because the sea is no longer around to warm up the land. But is it cold enough to actually *kill* the dinosaurs?

It may be that when the sea drained, all the plant life died out. That would have caused the plant-eaters to die—and without them to eat, the meat-eaters would have died too!

Then there's the darkened sky. That *also* may have been the cause of it all. Perhaps it was ash from a volcano, or a collision with a comet.

Your head is spinning. You feel that this trip is giving you more questions than answers!

Maybe if you slip back a few years, you can actually *see* what happened.

 Turn to page 81.

ou feel groggy and out of breath. There doesn't seem to be enough oxygen. You break out into a sweat and gulp the air as you lean against a tall rock for support.

You carefully scan the area for signs of life. You're by the shore of a lake. Behind you, flat, sparse land stretches in all directions—no dinosaurs, no mammals, no flowers. A few scraggly bushes and trees dot the horizon. Maybe you overshot the Great Extinction. You'd better head back in time.

Just as you're about to time-travel, you see movement underneath you. You look down to see an awkward-looking amphibian waddling between your legs.

The sight of this slimy creature takes you by surprise, and you let out a scream. But the amphibian doesn't react.

You're relieved that it looks so harmless. "Pretty brave, aren't you?" you say to it. Again, it doesn't respond to the sound of your voice.

This strikes you as strange. You clap your

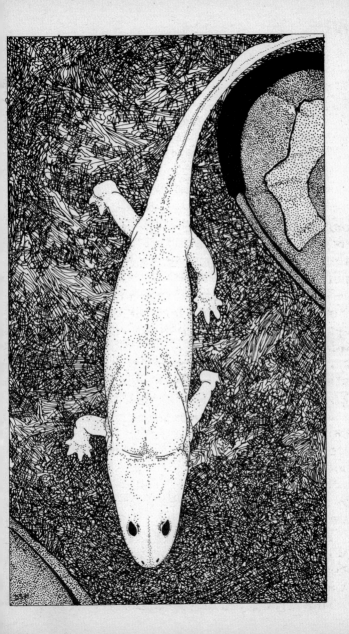

90

hands loudly. Still no reaction. In fact, when you look closely at its head, you can't see where its ears are. Is this some kind of mutant that survived the extinction?

It occurs to you that you've gone all the way back to the coal age, millions of years *before* the dinosaurs. And you're looking at one of the first life forms that ever walked the land—the *ichthyostega,* which is so primitive that it hasn't even developed hearing.

Suddenly you feel as if you're going to pass out. It occurs to you that you may be having trouble breathing because enough oxygen hasn't built up in the atmosphere this early in Earth's history.

You'd better jump quickly to the Great Extinction so you can complete your mission. But since you don't know exactly how far back in time you've gone, you're not sure how many years ahead you should travel!

 Try 300 million years ahead. Turn to page 96.

 Try 360 million years ahead. Turn to page 71.

You're blinded by whiteness all around you, and your teeth start to chatter. You have never been this cold in your life. The wind feels like knives against your skin. Can this place really be the same as the one you just traveled from?

You force your eyes open. Snow is falling furiously around you. Just as you think you're going to collapse, you hear several loud, sharp sounds.

You squint your eyes in the direction of the sounds. You see a moving black outline against the snow. As it gets closer, you realize it's a team of dogs pulling a sled! The dogs are barking loudly.

"It's . . . it's a human being!" you hear a voice shout. A group of men are trudging wearily behind the sled. One of them approaches you. His thick beard has so much ice on it, it looks as if it could break off from his face.

"P-p-please, sir," you say, shivering. "Do you have a coat I can wear?"

The man signals to one of the others, who pulls a huge fur wrap from the sled.

"Here," the man shouts through the deafening wind, as he takes the fur and hands it to you. "We've already lost a few of our men, so there are extra coats." His eyes are wide with astonishment. "How on Earth did you get here—and how did you survive dressed like that?"

You don't have the energy to think of a good alibi. "Uh . . . I g-got lost on the way to the s-ski lodge?"

"Ski lodge?" the man bellows. He turns to his companions and twirls his finger around near his head, as if to say that you're crazy. Then he puts his arm around your shoulder and says, "My name is Roald Amundsen, from Norway. What country are you from? I'd like to know who discovered the South Pole before me!"

You must be in the early twentieth century, in the middle of Antarctica. You've just convinced the discoverer of the South Pole that someone else beat him to it!

You remember that the polar caps didn't have ice until after the Mesozoic period. It was awfully warm where you came from—but right now you'd rather be there!

A huge blizzard is blowing your way. If you can stall Amundsen long enough, you'll be able to sneak away in the blinding storm.

"I haven't seen the South Pole at all," you say. "You see, Roald, it's like this . . ."

You're in luck. At that moment, the snowstorm explodes around you. The wind forces your new companions to close their eyes and turn their backs on you.

You are able to jump in time without being seen. Should you see what happened to the ocean creatures, or investigate the dinosaurs who lived on land instead?

Go back 65 million years to the Pacific Ocean. Turn to page 98.

Go back 65 million years to inland America. Turn to page 107.

he soot in the air is so heavy that it's stinging your eyes. You must have arrived sometime during the Great Extinction.

Maybe you can finish your mission now. If you're at the *end* of the extinction, you may be able to find the world's last dinosaur!

You see that you're on another cold mountaintop. You look out over an ocean. Your eyes follow the coastline as it disappears into the distance on your left. On your right, the mountains end, and so does the land. From the shape of the land, you realize you must be in the northwestern corner of North America, overlooking prehistoric Alaska!

You gaze down into the valley below. It's full of trees and plants, and the dinosaurs are alive and kicking. That means it must be fairly early in the Great Extinction. You're a little disappointed, and you prepare to jump ahead in time.

But something catches your eye. The outline of Alaska looks different from the maps you've seen. Instead of extending out into the Pacific with a group of small islands, it's actually *connected* with the Soviet Union. There's a long bridge of land that goes across the entire Pacific Ocean between the two continents!

Thousands of dinosaurs are crossing in either direction over the land bridge—triceratopses, duck-bills, tyrannosaurs, and more. Immediately you think of rinderpest.

Of course! *Now* you understand what killed off the yellow-spotted triceratopses. As with rinderpest, a new disease must have been brought to North America by dinosaurs from the other continent!

And there are so many dinosaurs crossing over, you wouldn't be surprised if *lots* of diseases are being spread!

You're ready to see the very end of the Great Extinction. If you push ahead a couple of million years, you'll probably hit it on the nose.

Go ahead two million years, into the valley you see below. Turn to page 109.

The sky is bright, yet you hear a sound like thunder. You look around the empty, grassy field—and freeze in fear.

That sound wasn't thunder at all. A herd of woolly beasts is heading right toward you! They are the ugliest things you've ever seen, with knobby heads that look like crushed soda cans. Their noses are pointed and wrinkled, beneath which two long tusks stick out.

You hurl yourself out of the way just in time and watch as they rumble into the distance. Those creatures couldn't be anything but mammals, you say to yourself. They run with their legs pointed straight ahead, so they're not from the Permian age. And they're the size of buffalo, not the small mammals you saw in the Cretaceous period. That can be only because there are no dinosaurs to kick them around anymore. You've *definitely* overshot the Great Extinction, this time.

But you're also witnessing the beginning of evolution in the Age of Mammals. In just a few million years, you'll be born!

You prepare to travel in time, as two more hairy, two-tusked beasts lumber onto the field. You recognize them as loxolophodons, and, as they lower their heads and charge toward each other, they look as though they've met to deal with some sort of personal problem.

There's nothing to help you with your mission here, so you jump in time to try to find the Great Extinction.

 Go back 70 million years. Turn to page 98.

You're sitting in wet sand that slopes upward. A horseshoe crab slides by you carried on a layer of water. You follow it with your eyes—and find yourself staring into a thirty-foot tidal wave!

You spring up and run as far away as you can. The wave crashes thunderously to the ground just behind you.

A safe distance from the shoreline, you stop to catch your breath. Trees lie all around you; it looks as if the tide has carried all the way into a forest. Lying in between the trees are sea lizards and plesiosaurs similar to the ones you met in the Jurassic sea. Washed up like this, they're not nearly as scary. In fact, most of them look as if they're dying. You wish you could do something for them.

As if it's reading your mind, a sea lizard that must be the length of five people opens its mouth at you. Well, *that's* not exactly what you had in mind!

You look back at the dark, swollen ocean. It makes sense that it's overflowing onto the

land—by now, at the end of the Cretaceous period, all the water from the inland sea has drained into it.

But if there's so much water, why are all the sea creatures dying?

Maybe there's something about the water that will give you a clue. You take off your shoes. Cautiously, you walk closer to the ocean. A few waves strike the shore, but none is as big as the one that almost did you in.

As soon as the water is fairly calm for a moment, you race down toward it. You won't have time before you're in danger again.

The water *looks* normal enough. You scoop some up with your hand and taste it. It's salt water, all right. But you notice that your hand is numb. You stick a foot in the water. Immediately the cold makes you jerk it back.

That's why the creatures are dying! When the inland seas drained into the ocean, they made the oceans much deeper and must have caused the water's temperature to drop. The fish, lizards and plesiosaurs are freezing to death!

You've found *another* possible cause of the Great Extinction. No wonder it's so hard for scientists to figure all this out!

Water is sweeping the ground clean around the bodies. You need to find a tooth to take home, but you'd be more likely to find it inland. You decide that it would be best to go into the middle of North America—but you don't want to pass the Great Extinction, so you'll travel ahead only a couple of thousand years.

Turn to page 107.

You're standing on a foothill of a high mountain range. You look down, but there's not much to see. The air is dark and smoggy. A freezing wind lashes your face, and you shiver. This is the coldest you've been on your trip. You head down the mountain.

As you approach the bottom, you're met by a horrible sight. Corpses of tyrannosaurs, triceratopses, and duck-bills are lying all around. Some of them look as if they've been attacked, but most of them show no signs of injury at all. They're just thin and wrinkled, as though they starved to death.

It's no wonder, you realize. There are no plants around, and just about every tree is barren. The temperature is cool even down here, and the land is dry and cracked. The dinosaurs couldn't possibly survive in these conditions. It looks as if you've arrived after the Great Extinction.

But you're wrong; now you see that there are still signs of life. A bone-thin duck-bill wobbles over to you on unsteady legs. It looks at you with bloodshot eyes and blows a pathetic little toot from its horn. You feel sorry for it and reach into your pockets for something to feed it. The only thing you can find is a candy bar that's become soggy from having been in the Jurassic sea.

You hold it out to the duck-bill, and it leans down to take a sniff. In disappointment, it walks away.

"This is no time to be polite! Take it!" you say. But the dinosaur goes over to examine a dry bush. Of course! You realize that duck-bills are plant-eaters; they don't have much use for chocolate caramel.

But something else does. You hear a loud squawk above you, and a pair of claws grasps the candy bar out of your hand. You jump back as a large bird flies away with it toward a low ridge.

Staring after it, you wonder if it really *is* a bird. It doesn't have a beak, and when it opens its mouth to squawk, you see rows of teeth. It's more like a flying dinosaur. It must be a Late Cretaceous *ichthyornis*.

You wonder where it's going.

Follow it over the ridge. Turn to page 84.

The first things you notice are the vultures circling hungrily above you. You wave at them to make sure they know you're not dead. Then you brush yourself off, stand up, and look around the jungle clearing.

The ground is littered with bodies, again. But this time they're antelopes! You must have hopped way into the future.

In one corner of the clearing is a wagon the size of a pickup truck. Two horses are tethered to the front of it. Next to the wagon, a man in a cotton mesh hat is writing something on a piece of paper. He seems to be counting the antelope while other men load them onto the wagon.

You try to duck behind a tree, but he sees you. "You there!" he calls out with a British accent. "Come out from hiding!"

"Who is it, warden?" one of his helpers asks him.

"I couldn't tell," the man answers. "It must be someone from the new missionary's family." Then he yells to you again, "Come on out, you little scamp!"

Good—he thinks he knows who you are. You walk out from behind the tree.

"Got bored with your dad's sermonizing, eh?" the warden says with a wink. Then he turns back to his work. "We've got to lug these poor beasts away so the vultures will stay out of the settlement. Want to help?"

"No, thanks," you reply, watching the workmen drag the animals over to the truck. "What happened to them sir?"

"Rinderpest," the man says.

"Sorry. Uh . . . what happened to them, Mr. Rinderpest?"

The man throws back his head and roars with laughter. "No, no! They've died of the rinderpest *disease!* Haven't you heard of it?"

You look at him blankly.

"I thought *all* of Africa knew about rinderpest!" he continues, shaking his head in disbelief. "It's the worst plague that ever hit the wildlife here. By now, perhaps a million antelope and cattle have been killed!"

"How did it start?" you ask.

The warden thinks back. "About twenty years ago, in the 1880s or '90s, Lord Kitchener of England needed to haul cannons up the Nile to fight a battle. To do the job, he brought cattle from India."

"And *they* had rinderpest!"

"Precisely! The disease was unknown in Africa until then, and it spread like wildfire." He sighs. "Lord Kitchener did not know that animals should always stay in their habitats, because their diseases will sometimes spread especially fast in a new environment."

You begin to think of the triceratopses. Maybe something similar to rinderpest happened during the Late Cretaceous period.

The warden excuses himself and goes back to the wagon. You wander off into the woods and slip into time.

Go back to the Great Extinction. Turn to page 94.

ou recognize this setting. The sky is dark and sooty, and you're in the middle of a dried-out swamp. There are still some trees and plants around, but not many. It sounds as if there's a brass band behind you. You think you know what that is, too.

Sure enough, you turn around to see scores of duck-billed dinosaurs tooting away. Some of them are blowing through long tubes on their heads. Others have large crests that look like hats. Still others have just a hole, surrounded by a big lump, above their eyes.

Someone ought to tune them up. You put your fingers to your ears.

As you expected, there are dinosaur bodies scattered all around. But they're not the dinosaurs you thought they'd be. It seems that many of the meat-eaters are dying off, while the plant-eating duck-bills are still alive.

Until now, you thought the plant-eaters died first, after the soot choked off sunlight and caused the plants to die. What could have caused these meat-eaters to die first? After all, there seem to be enough duck-bills around for them to eat.

You walk over to one of the dead dinosaurs. You notice its skin is puffy and covered with yellow spots. It looks like some sort of disease. You see that the other bodies have spots, too.

Once again, you seem to have found a reason for the Great Extinction. In this area of the world a disease is spreading that appears to affect only one type of dinosaur. Maybe other diseases are around, too.

You back away from the body and hear a roar behind you. Spinning around, you see another triceratops. It's covered with spots, but it's still alive. And it's charging toward you like a wounded bull.

There's no time to think; just jump blindly into time.

 Turn to page 104.

ou made it! There's no mistaking that this is the end of the Great Extinction. The sky is practically black with soot, and the air is so cold that you can see your breath. Every tree that remains standing is a shriveled mass of gray branches. Foul-smelling smoke rises up from a huge, distant hole in the ground, and there isn't one live dinosaur around.

You've solved one part of your mission—the time of the Great Extinction was a little less than 65 million years B.C. Despite the destruction around you, you feel a sense of accomplishment.

Suddenly a sharp *ccrrrraacck* disrupts the eerie silence. You look behind you to see an enormous tree about to flatten you. You've been in *this* predicament before!

You dive away as the tree slams downward onto the parched ground and sends up a cloud of dust. Instantly, a tiny mammal appears and scurries to the tree. Working quickly, it picks off all the dried-out berries and acorns it can

find. Like a squirrel, it stores everything in a pouch in its mouth and scampers back to its hole.

You watch the little animal and smile. "Congratulations," you say to it, softly, knowing that only small mammals will survive and that they will eventually evolve into human beings. It's hard to imagine that that little furball may be your great-great-grandparent, 65 million years removed!

You sigh to yourself. You couldn't solve the mystery of the Great Extinction for certain, but you've seen a lot of possible reasons why it happened. And that may have to be enough.

Then you're struck by an idea. Your mission isn't a failure at all. Maybe you *have* discovered the great secret. Maybe *all* of the things you saw worked together to cause the extinction.

Just then your eye is caught by a moving white object. Next to the body of a triceratops, an egg is hatching. You watch as the little horned creature struggles to its feet. It steadies itself on unsure legs and nudges its motionless mama. It seems upset that she doesn't respond. With fear and bewilderment in its eyes, it tosses back its head and gives out a little bellow of hunger.

You know this creature will not be able to survive for long. You didn't think it would be so painful to see the last dinosaur on Earth. You feel like taking it back to the twentieth

century, but you know that's against the rules of time travel.

Your mission has been a success, but your feeling of triumph is mixed with sadness. On the ground you see a large tooth that has long since broken off a dinosaur. You pick it up and head back home.

MISSION COMPLETED.

DATA FILE

Page 44: How many years ago did the dinosaurs first appear on the Earth?

Page 52: One of the main ideas about evolution will help you: survival of the fittest.

Page 58: What was much of the earth's land like in the Jurassic period?

Page 62: There was lots of screeching in the Mesozoic period, but no metal—although some things were armored!

Page 67: Where will you be if you're wrong?

Page 72: Would it be better to go too far in time or not far enough?

Page 83: What's hot in the Mesozoic may not be in the future.

Page 90: How many years ago was the coal age?

About the Contributors

PETER LERANGIS is an author, actor, singer, and teacher. He has had over a dozen books published, including Time Traveler #4, *The Amazing Ben Franklin,* and Explorer #3, *In Search of a Shark.* He wrote the storybook adaptations for the movies *Young Sherlock Holmes, Little Shop of Horrors,* and *Star Trek IV.* He has been in the Broadway show *They're Playing Our Song* and has played lead roles in many shows throughout the country.

DOUG HENDERSON is a respected illustrator and fine artist whose depictions of the Mesozoic Era have won the admiration of paleontologists and aficionados of natural history art. He did a children's book with dinosaur expert Jack Horner and continues to research his favorite subject at the sites of dinosaur digs. He currently resides in Montana.